MR. SNOW

by Roger Hargreaves

D0485272

One night, two days before Christmas, it started to snow.

All night it snowed and snowed and snowed and snowed and snowed.

Millions and billions and trillions of big, white, soft snowflakes covered the whole, wide world.

When morning came it was quite amazing to see just how much snow had fallen.

All the houses, all the trees, all the roads and all the fields were covered.

It was almost as if a huge, white blanket had been gently laid over everything.

Everywhere you looked was white!

And then the sun came out!

And so did the children!

They were all dressed up and muffled up, wearing scarves and woollies and gloves and boots so that they wouldn't catch cold.

All the children were so excited to see so much snow, which isn't surprising really because there was more snow than they'd ever seen before.

Some of them went on their sledges, racing down the hills.

Some of them, who didn't have sledges, threw snowballs at each other.

One little boy even made a snowball that was as big as himself.

And some of the children made snowmen!

Then it was Christmas Eve.

The children all went home early so that they could go to bed early so that they could get up early to see what Father Christmas had brought them.

But that particular Christmas Eve, Father Christmas was in trouble.

And the trouble was that it had snowed so much that Father Christmas was stuck.

Well and truly stuck!

There was so much snow that his reindeer simply couldn't pull his sleigh piled high with all the presents that he had to deliver to all the children.

"Oh dear!" thought Father Christmas to himself. "Oh dear me. What am I to do?"

He sat down on his sack of toys and thought and thought how he could manage to deliver all the presents to all the children before they woke up on Christmas morning.

"Oh dear! Oh dear me!" he said out loud, and sighed.

Now, it just so happened that Father Christmas had got himself stuck just beside a snowman which one of the children had built.

And that gave him an idea.

A good idea.

A very good idea.

A very good idea indeed.

"How would you like to help me?" he asked the snowman.

But of course the snowman didn't answer because snowmen can't talk, can they?

"Of course, I'll have to use some of my magic to bring him to life," thought Father Christmas to himself.

So, he tugged his white beard three times and muttered some Father Christmassy magic words into it.

Suddenly, you might almost say magically, the snowman did come to life.

"Hello Father Christmas," said Mr Snow, which was the snowman's name.

"You look a bit sort of stuck if you ask me, which you aren't , but I'll say so anyway, and if you ask me again I'd say you need a sort of helping hand, if you know what I mean, which you probably do, because that's probably why you've brought me to life, which you certainly did, so can I be of any assistance?"

Mr Snow, as you might have gathered, was a rather talkative sort of snowman.

"Exactly!" beamed Father Christmas. "Let's get started!"

And start they did.

Mr Snow gave Father Christmas an enormous push, and off they went.

They divided the work between them.

It was Mr Snow's job to make sure that all the right toys for all the right boys, and all the right toys for all the right girls, were put into all the right sacks.

It was Father Christmas's job to make sure he took all the right sacks down all the right chimneys and delivered all the right toys to all the right boys and all the right toys to all the right girls.

Mr Snow and Father Christmas made sure that Susan got her teddy bear.

Mr Snow and Father Christmas made sure that Peter got his train.

Mr Snow and Father Christmas made sure that John got his piggy bank.

Mr Snow and Father Christmas even made sure that little Jane got her squeaky, pink elephant to play with in the bath.

And then, all of a sudden, they discovered that, between them, they'd finished.

"I'd like to thank you very much indeed for helping me deliver all the right toys to all the right boys," said Father Christmas, shaking Mr Snow by the hand.

"Not forgetting all the right toys to all the right girls," replied Mr Snow, shaking Father Christmas by the hand.

"And now I'd better turn you back into a snowman again," said Father Christmas.

"Thank you again and goodbye!"

"My pleasure!" smiled Mr Snow.

And do you know, from that Christmas to this Christmas, Father Christmas always chooses a snowman to help him.

So the next time you build a snowman, you'd better make sure you build him properly, because somebody you know might want that snowman to give him a hand.

And you know who that would be, don't you?

CUT ALONG DOTTED LINE AND RETURN THIS WHOLE PAGE

3 Great Offers for MR. MEN Fans!

MR. MEN TOKEN

1 New Mr. Men or Little Miss Library Bus Presentation Cases

A brand new stronger, roomier school bus library box, with sturdy carrying handle and stay-closed fasteners.
The full colour, wipe-clean boxes make a great home for your full collection.
They're just £5.99 inc P&P and free bookmark!

☐ MR. MEN   ☐ LITTLE MISS (please tick and order overleaf)

2 Door Hangers and Posters

In every Mr. Men and Little Miss book like this one, you will find a special token. Collect 6 tokens and we will send you a brilliant Mr. Men or Little Miss poster and a Mr. Men or Little Miss double sided full colour bedroom door hanger of your choice. Simply tick your choice in the list and tape a 50p coin for your two items to this page.

PLEASE STICK YOUR 50P COIN HERE

Door Hangers (please tick)
☐ Mr. Nosey & Mr. Muddle
☐ Mr. Slow & Mr. Busy
☐ Mr. Messy & Mr. Quiet
☐ Mr. Perfect & Mr. Forgetful
☐ Little Miss Fun & Little Miss Late
☐ Little Miss Helpful & Little Miss Tidy
☐ Little Miss Busy & Little Miss Brainy
☐ Little Miss Star & Little Miss Fun

Posters (please tick)
☐ MR. MEN
☐ LITTLE MISS

3 Sixteen Beautiful Fridge Magnets – any 2 for £2.00! inc.P&P

They're very special collector's items!
Simply tick your first and second* choices from the list below
of any 2 characters!

1st Choice

- ☐ Mr. Happy
- ☐ Mr. Lazy
- ☐ Mr. Topsy-Turvy
- ☐ Mr. Bounce
- ☐ Mr. Bump
- ☐ Mr. Small
- ☐ Mr. Snow
- ☐ Mr. Wrong

- ☐ Mr. Daydream
- ☐ Mr. Tickle
- ☐ Mr. Greedy
- ☐ Mr. Funny
- ☐ Little Miss Giggles
- ☐ Little Miss Splendid
- ☐ Little Miss Naughty
- ☐ Little Miss Sunshine

2nd Choice

- ☐ Mr. Happy
- ☐ Mr. Lazy
- ☐ Mr. Topsy-Turvy
- ☐ Mr. Bounce
- ☐ Mr. Bump
- ☐ Mr. Small
- ☐ Mr. Snow
- ☐ Mr. Wrong

- ☐ Mr. Daydream
- ☐ Mr. Tickle
- ☐ Mr. Greedy
- ☐ Mr. Funny
- ☐ Little Miss Giggles
- ☐ Little Miss Splendid
- ☐ Little Miss Naughty
- ☐ Little Miss Sunshine

*Only in case your first choice is out of stock.

— TO BE COMPLETED BY AN ADULT —

**To apply for any of these great offers, ask an adult to complete the coupon below and send it with
the appropriate payment and tokens, if needed, to MR. MEN CLASSIC OFFER, PO BOX 715, HORSHAM RH12 5WG**

☐ Please send _____ Mr. Men Library case(s) and/or _____ Little Miss Library case(s) at £5.99 each inc P&P

☐ Please send a poster and door hanger as selected overleaf. I enclose six tokens plus a 50p coin for P&P

☐ Please send me _____ pair(s) of Mr. Men/Little Miss fridge magnets, as selected above at £2.00 inc P&P

Fan's Name _____

Address _____

_____ **Postcode** _____

Date of Birth _____

Name of Parent/Guardian _____

Total amount enclosed £ _____

☐ **I enclose a cheque/postal order payable to Egmont Books Limited**

☐ **Please charge my MasterCard/Visa/Amex/Switch or Delta account** (delete as appropriate)

Card Number

Expiry date ___/___   **Signature** _____

Please allow 28 days for delivery. Offer is only available while stocks last. We reserve the right to change the terms
of this offer at any time and we offer a 14 day money back guarantee. This does not affect your statutory rights.
Data Protection Act: If you do not wish to receive other similar offers from us or companies we recommend, please
tick this box ☐. Offers apply to UK only.

MR. MEN   LITTLE MISS
Mr. Men and Little Miss™ & ©Mrs. Roger Hargreaves

CUT ALONG DOTTED LINE AND RETURN THIS WHOLE PAGE